BENJAMIN BEAR

IN

FUZZY THINKING

A TOON BOOK BY

PHILIPPE COUDRAY

TOON BOOKS IS AN IMPRINT OF CANDLEWICK PRESS

AN EISNER AWARD NOMINEE
Best Publication for Early Readers

A JUNIOR LIBRARY GUILD SELECTION

For Robert, Debbie, and their children

Editorial Director: FRANÇOISE MOULY

Book Design: FRANÇOISE MOULY & JONATHAN BENNETT

Translation: LEIGH STEIN

PHILIPPE COUDRAY'S artwork was drawn in india ink and colored digitally.

A TOON Book™ © 2011 RAW Junior, LLC, 27 Greene Street, New York, NY 10013. TOON Books® is an imprint of Candlewick Press, 99 Dover Street, Somerville, MA 02144. Original French text and art © 2010 Philippe Coudray and La Boîte à Bulles. No part of this book may be used or reproduced in any manner whatsoever without written permission except in the case of brief quotations embodied in critical articles and reviews. TOON Books®, LITTLE LIT® and TOON Into Reading!™ are trademarks of RAW Junior, LLC. All rights reserved. Printed in Dongguan, Guangdong, China by Toppan Leefung. The Library of Congress has cataloged the hardcover edition as follows:

Coudray, Philippe.   Benjamin Bear in Fuzzy thinking : a TOON book / by Philippe Coudray.

    p. cm.   Summary: Although he is a very serious bear, Benjamin Bear has a funny way of doing things, like drying dishes on a rabbit's back or sharing his sweater without taking it off.   ISBN: 978-1-935179-12-2 (hardcover)

1. Graphic novels. [1. Graphic novels. 2. Bears–Fiction. 3. Humorous stories.] I. Title. II. Title: Fuzzy thinking.

PZ7.7.C68Be 2011   741.5'973–dc22   2011000801

ISBN: 978-1-935179-25-2 (paperback)

13 14 15 16 17 18 TPN 10 9 8 7 6 5 4 3 2 1

www.TOON-BOOKS.com

A big fish

Cold night

Painting

Tall tree

Philippe Coudray

Karate

Philippe Coudray

To fly—or not

Philippe Coudray

10

A long nap

The man in the moon

Underwater

The maze

Help your friends

Play with me

philippe Coudray

To jump—or not

Philippe Coudray

17

Sailboat

18

At the store

Philippe Coudray

Sunset

Winter is coming

Too much wind!

Philippe Coudray

22

The winner

Philippe Coudray

23

A good friend

Philippe Coudray

24

Do as you are told!

Philippe Coudray

25

Friends

The biggest fish

I want to play!

The hot dog

Back to school

The comic strip

THE END

ABOUT THE AUTHOR

PHILIPPE COUDRAY loves drawing comics, and his many children's books are often used in the schools of France, his home country. In fact, his work was chosen by students to win the prestigious Angoulême Prix des Écoles. Philippe's twin brother Jean-Luc is also a humorist, and they relish any opportunity to collaborate on children's books and comics. Although he lives in Bordeaux, Philippe does not especially like wine. He does enjoy painting, creating stereoscopic images, and traveling to Canada, where he looks for Bigfoot. Though he continues to search each year, Benjamin Bear will always be his favorite wild animal.

HOW TO "TOON INTO READING"
in a few simple steps:

Our goal is to get kids reading—and we know kids LOVE comics.
We publish award-winning early readers in comics form for
elementary and early middle school, and present them in three levels.

 FIND THE RIGHT BOOK

Veteran teacher Cindy Rosado tells what makes
a good book for beginning and struggling
readers alike: "A vetted vocabulary, plenty of
picture clues, repetition, and a clear and
compelling story. Also, the book shouldn't be
too easy—or the reader won't learn, but neither
should it be too hard—or he or she may
get discouraged."

*If you love Benjamin, look for more of his
adventures in "Bright Ideas!"*

**BENJAMIN BEAR
in Bright Ideas!**
by Philippe Coudray

The **TOON INTO READING!**™
program is designed for beginning
readers and works wonders with
reluctant readers.

 TAKE TIME WITH SILENT PANELS

Comics use panels to mark time, and silent panels count. Look and "read"
even when there are no words. Often, humor is all in the timing!

3 GUIDE YOUNG READERS

What works?
Keep your fingertip <u>below</u> the character that is speaking.

4 LET THE PICTURES TELL THE STORY

In a comic, you can often read the story even if you don't know all the words. Encourage young readers to tell you what's happening based on the facial expressions and body language.

Get kids talking, and you'll be surprised at how perceptive they are about pictures.

5 GET OUT THE CRAYONS

Kids see the hand of the author in a comic and it makes them want to tell their own stories. Encourage them to talk, write and draw!

6 LET THEM GUESS

Comics provide a large amount of context for the words, so let young readers make informed guesses, and don't over-correct. In this panel, the artist shows a pirate ship, two pirate hats, and two pirate flags the first time the word "PIRATE" is introduced.

3 1901 05314 7593